This book belongs to:

The English Roses

Too Good To Be True

by

Madonna

Illustrated by
Stacy Peterson

CALLAWAY
New York
2006

This book is dedicated to orphans everywhere.

I f you haven't heard of the English Roses by now, then you are either:

    a. Living under a rock.

    b. Living on the moon.

    c. Away with the fairies.

If you fit the description of a, b, or c, then I am happy to clue you in to what the rest of the world already knows.

The English Roses are five girls named Nicole, Amy, Charlotte, Grace, and Binah. They're best friends who do everything together:

Dancing,

homework,

ice-skating,

picnics,

sleepover parties. . . .

Oh, fiddlesticks! If I go on and on then I won't get to the rest of the story! Now, where was I? Oh yes, the English Roses. Well, there was a time when they were four, not five.

It was all because of the BIG GREEN MONSTER! She came waltzing into their lives, totally uninvited.

You see, the other girls treated Binah as if she did not exist because they thought she was too pretty, and too smart, and too perfect.

But what she really was, was too lonely.

Fortunately, their friendly fairy godmother made them invisible with magic fairy dust and they were able to observe Binah's life without being noticed. What they found was very far from perfect. They realized that they had misjudged Binah and decided to stop acting like silly, selfish ninnies and be her friend. So Binah became an English Rose, too, and they all lived happily ever after.

Or did they?

Well, as you know, once you work out one problem in life, another one comes along and tries to throw a bucket of worms in your pants.

This is where our story begins.

It was the first day of school, and the English Roses were excited to be starting fifth grade. They rushed to get there on time, carrying their new book bags and wearing their favorite outfits.

Their new teacher's name was Miss Fluffernutter. She had a pile of gray fluff on her head that had a mind of its own. Her outfits never seemed to match and she was not what you'd call fashionable, but everyone loved her because she was beautiful on the inside. She also had a reputation for making work fun. During cleanup, she had been known to put on funky music and encourage the class to dance while they worked. Sometimes she would jump on her desk and burst into song. The English Roses couldn't wait to have fun with her!

A fter the bell rang, Miss Fluffernutter began to call out the students' names. She came to a name that no one had ever heard before:

Dominic de la Guardia

It sounded like a poem or a symphony. A voice with a foreign accent said, "Present." Everyone turned around.

Have you ever seen anything that was T.G.T.B.T.?
Well, that's what Dominic de la Guardia was:
Too Good To Be True.
Every girl's heart skipped a beat.

Head in the clouds...

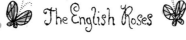

...fluttery tummy...

Wait a second. Hadn't the English Roses already learned that valuable lesson?

Well, smarty-pants, sometimes a lesson needs to be learned more than once. Now, stop interrupting me!

Dominic turned out to be an exchange student from Spain. He would be living for a year with the Ferguson family, Amy's neighbors.

Not only was he nice, but he was also smart, and he had excellent manners. He was also a great soccer player (just thought I'd mention it).

He was kind of, well, perfect. Oops, there's that word again; that scary, intimidating, impossible-to-live-up-to word: perfect.

The English Roses were in a constant state of competition with one another. They didn't do it on purpose. They didn't mean to like the same boy. They just couldn't help themselves.

...weak knees...

tongue tied...

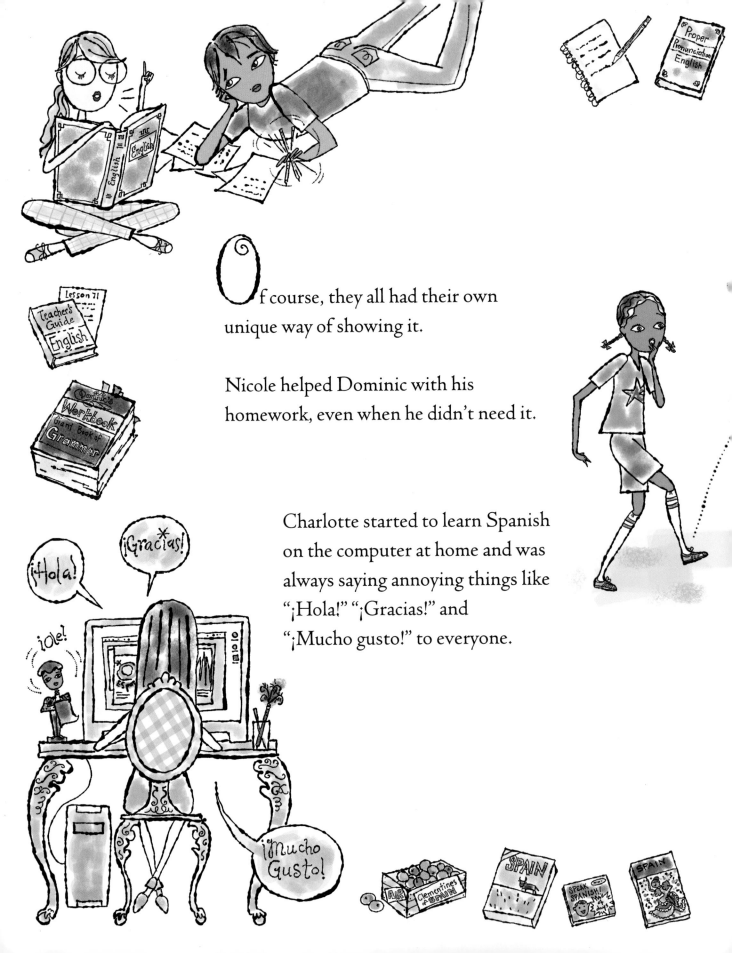

Of course, they all had their own unique way of showing it.

Nicole helped Dominic with his homework, even when he didn't need it.

Charlotte started to learn Spanish on the computer at home and was always saying annoying things like "¡Hola!" "¡Gracias!" and "¡Mucho gusto!" to everyone.

Amy spent even more time in front of the mirror than usual, choosing the perfect outfit and futzing with her hair.

And Grace talked about sports incessantly. She even carried a soccer ball in her bag, just in case he wanted to play.

The only person who didn't seem interested in Dominic was Binah. She was too busy worrying about her papa and getting all her work done. She didn't have time to moon over good-looking boys.

One day, Miss Fluffernutter announced that the fall dance was only a week away. As fifth graders, they were finally old enough to attend. She asked if anyone in class would like to stay after school and help make decorations for the gymnasium, where the dance would be held. The English Roses all raised their hands at the same time. Because that's what best friends do: they think alike.

Well, at least most of the time.

Dominic de la Guardia raised his hand, too. The English Roses all sighed with approval.

....like peas in a pod....

After school, the gym was full of volunteers from fifth through eighth grade. Miss Fluffernutter put music on and ran around listening to suggestions, helping out, and getting everyone excited. She loved Dominic's suggestion to make a piñata.

Charlotte and Nicole volunteered to help him build the papier-mâché animal. Amy said she'd bring records and be the DJ. Grace and Miss Fluffernutter decided to make daisy chains to run from one end of the room to the other. Binah sat down to draw posters to hang in the halls.

Every once in a while, Dominic would stop his work to chat with Binah and see if she needed any help. Binah would always say, "No, but thanks for asking." The rest of the Roses were slightly alarmed that he had not offered his help to anyone else.

You are probably wondering if the world just revolved around the English Roses. Well, sometimes they thought it did. But, in fact, it did not.

Did I mention Bunny Love and Candy Darling? They were twin sisters in the sixth grade. They lived in a house that looked like it belonged to Hansel and Gretel. They'd been tap-dancing since they were five, and by now they were practically professionals. They asked Miss Fluffernutter if they could perform their new routine for the party.

Miss Fluffernutter thought it was a smashing idea, and Bunny and Candy practically danced all the way home to tell their mother the news.

The week flew by, and every day the English Roses would help Miss Fluffernutter and the other students decorate.

Every day, Dominic de la Guardia would stop his work on the piñata and walk over to Binah's table to sit down and talk to her.

Sometimes, he told her funny stories about his village in Spain. Every time Binah laughed, the other Roses felt a little squeeze on their hearts.

A tiny tug of indignation. A little prickling of perturbedness (I know, I know, that's not a word, but I'm telling the story around here, and I can use any word I want).

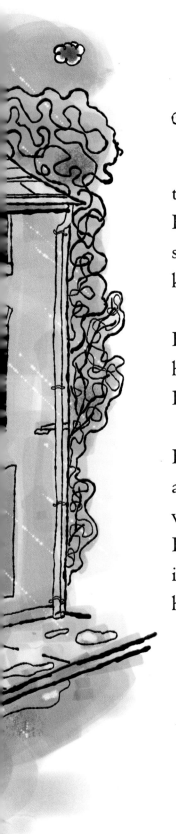

By the end of the week, the gymnasium looked totally different. But something was different about the English Roses, too. They had stopped asking Binah if she needed any help at home with her chores, and they kept forgetting to walk with her to school.

Binah was sad and confused. She could see what was happening, but she did not know what to do. She liked Dominic, but she did not want to upset her best friends.

Binah asked her dad what she should do, and he encouraged her to be honest with her friends about her feelings. He suggested that it might be a good idea to ask Miss Fluffernutter for her advice as well.

During class, Miss Fluffernutter could tell something was bothering Binah. After the bell rang, she gave her a big hug and said, "There is no problem that cannot be solved. Let's meet in my office."

After the class filed out, Binah and Dominic were the only ones left behind. Dominic walked over to Binah's desk, smiled his beautiful smile, and said, "Would you like me to walk home with you?"

Binah felt nervous and bit her lip. "No, thanks. I have a meeting with Miss Fluffernutter," she replied.

Dominic looked a bit disappointed. "Are you going to the dance tonight?" he asked.

"Of course I am, silly. After all that work, I wouldn't miss it for the world!"

"Ah, good," sighed Dominic as he ran out the door. "See you there!"

In Miss Fluffernutter's office, Binah noticed several pictures of a man with a very kind face.

"Is that someone in your family?" Binah asked.

"Yes," replied Miss Fluffernutter. "That is my husband. He died several years ago, and even though he's no longer with me in a way that I can see him, he is always in my heart."

"That's what I say about my mother," said Binah. "She died when I was little. Sometimes I miss her so much. You must miss your husband, too."

"Indeed, I do. That's why I've decided to try and be happy all the time. Even the things we think are difficult are really blessings in disguise. They are given to us so that we can learn lessons from them."

"Well, I guess that's why I am here," said Binah. "I need to know how to handle a certain situation, and I am not sure what I am supposed to be learning from it."

Miss Fluffernutter was all ears.

Binah told her the whole story of the English Roses. How they had been wonderful and kind in the past year. How Dominic's arrival had made them act differently toward her. How they were no longer calling her or coming over to help her with her chores.

"Mmm, I see," mused Miss Fluffernutter, sitting and thinking for a moment. "Sounds like the BIG GREEN MONSTER to me," she said. "She's a tricky one."

She explained that the other girls were not angry with Binah, but at the attention she was getting. "I think I know exactly what needs to be done. Now run along and get ready!"

Sssssss

Miss Fluffernutter remembered that there were several brothers in the Ferguson house, where Dominic was staying. There was Timmy, Terry, and the twins, Taffy and Tricky.

That's a real tongue twister if you say it fast enough. Go on, say it fast enough:

Timmy, Terry, Taffy, Tricky.
Timmy, Terry, Taffy, Tricky.
Timmy, Terry, Taffy, Tricky.
Timmy, Terry, Taffy, Tricky.

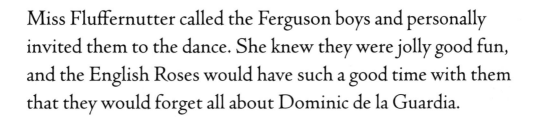

How do you think Mrs. Ferguson feels?

Now, where was I? Oh, yes—the plan.

Miss Fluffernutter called the Ferguson boys and personally invited them to the dance. She knew they were jolly good fun, and the English Roses would have such a good time with them that they would forget all about Dominic de la Guardia.

"No problem at all, Miss Fluffernutter," said Timmy, the oldest boy. "We might need to bring our dad to play the fiddle. Would that be all right?"

"Fiddle-dee-dee!" exclaimed Miss Fluffernutter. "That's the all-rightiest thing I've heard in a long time!"

After Binah had finished her chores, she looked in her closet for something to wear to the dance. But all she found were sensible skirts and blouses like the ones she always wore.

"That's all right," she said, and smiled to herself. "I'll tie a ribbon in my hair and wear some new socks."

"You'll do nothing of the sort!" came a voice from out of nowhere.

Binah turned around, and there stood a plump woman with spectacles falling off her nose. She was eating a pumpernickel sandwich.

"Who are you?" asked Binah, who, unlike the other English Roses, had never met a fairy godmother before.

"I am your fairy godmother, silly. Now look, we haven't got much time. A fairy friend has outgrown this lovely dress and I'm a little too . . . well, it's not really my color, is it? I thought maybe you could use it."

She handed Binah a pale pink dress covered with tiny polka dots.

"It's . . . it's . . . it's beautiful!" exclaimed Binah. "I don't know what to say."

"A simple 'thank you' will do, and I'll be on my way," said the persnickety fairy godmother. "I'm a very busy woman, and my services are in great demand."

"Thank you," said Binah, as politely as she could, and the fairy godmother disappeared.

ZAP!

Binah's new dress fit perfectly. It was the prettiest dress she had ever seen, and she felt so special wearing it. She kissed her father good-bye and ran out the door to find Grace, who lived next door.

"Would you like to walk with me to the dance, Grace?" she asked her.

"Um, I guess so," said Grace, remembering that she was supposed to be angry with Binah. But in her heart, she didn't really want to be. And besides, she thought to herself, she is just so darned nice.

Grace swooped out the door, grabbing Binah's hand. "Let's get out of here before we miss all the fun!"

When they arrived, the dance was in full swing.
The gymnasium looked like a beautiful garden
had suddenly taken root in it. There were flowers
and trees everywhere, and there was even a big
swing in the corner. Amy was spinning records
and lots of kids were dancing.

Miss Fluffernutter was standing behind a long
table that held refreshments and snacks. She was
dressed like Heidi from Switzerland, except that
Heidi probably didn't own pink high-top sneakers
and a long feather boa.

When Miss Fluffernutter saw the girls arrive, she went over to say hello to Binah and Grace. "You girls look lovely!" she said, beaming at them.

"So do you, Miss Fluffernutter," Binah replied.

"I love your feather boa!" Grace added.

"I am just itching to dance," said Miss Fluffernutter. "I'm going to ask Dominic de la Guardia to spin me around the dance floor."

The girls giggled and ran off to find the rest of the English Roses, who were on the other side of the room, laughing and talking to the Ferguson boys.

Dominic de la Guardia was quite a spiffy dancer, but all eyes were on Miss Fluffernutter. She was dancing like a whirling dervish.

When they'd finished, Dominic came over to ask Binah to dance, and though she wanted to more than anything, she said no out of loyalty to the English Roses.

The Ferguson brothers grabbed the rest of the girls and hit the floor, leaving Binah all by herself.

Care to dance, Luv?

Charlotte looked up from the dance floor and noticed Binah standing alone. She turned and saw Dominic on the other side of the room standing by himself as well. In the blink of an eye, she realized how unfair the English Roses had been to Binah—again.

efore Charlotte could do
anything about it, Miss Fluffernutter
jumped up onstage and announced that
there would be two special performances.

Everyone took a seat on the floor.
This time, Charlotte insisted that
Binah sit next to Dominic, which put
a very big smile on Binah's face.

It was time for the show to begin.

Bunny and Candy had choreographed a tap dance to their favorite song. They were dressed like sailors, and they did everything in unison: splits and jumps and cartwheels and turns. They did it with precision and perfect timing. You couldn't tell one twin from the other. It was very impressive.

When the number was over, Miss Fluffernutter was up on her feet again asking everyone for quiet so the Ferguson boys could begin their jig.

Tippity Tap Tippity Tap Tap Tap!

The Ferguson boys stomped their feet and
clapped their hands and swung each other
around by the arms. Pretty soon, the whole
room was clapping and stomping, too.

Taffy and Tricky did flips and acrobatics, and
Timmy and Terry did some pretty fancy footwork.

Old Mr. Ferguson played a mean fiddle.
They were quite a family. They got a
standing ovation when they were finished.

The English Roses had the time of their lives, and they couldn't wait to tell the Fergusons how good they were when they came offstage. Then they congratulated Bunny Love and Candy Darling and asked them to go bowling that weekend.

"We'd love to!" answered the twins simultaneously.

When the dance ended, the English Roses stayed to help clean up.

So did Dominic de la Guardia.

So did the Ferguson brothers.

So did Miss Fluffernutter's feather boa. It collected more dust than her broom!

When all the chairs were stacked and the floor was swept, the English Roses thanked Miss Fluffernutter for a great night. She hugged the girls and reminded them how important it was to cherish one another.

"I've got an idea!" she whispered. "The next time you start to feel jealous of someone, try to feel happy for them instead. Good things will come your way, too. It will be hard at first, but are the English Roses afraid of a challenge?"

"No way!" they shouted together.

"That's my girls!" said Miss Fluffernutter, hugging them all again.

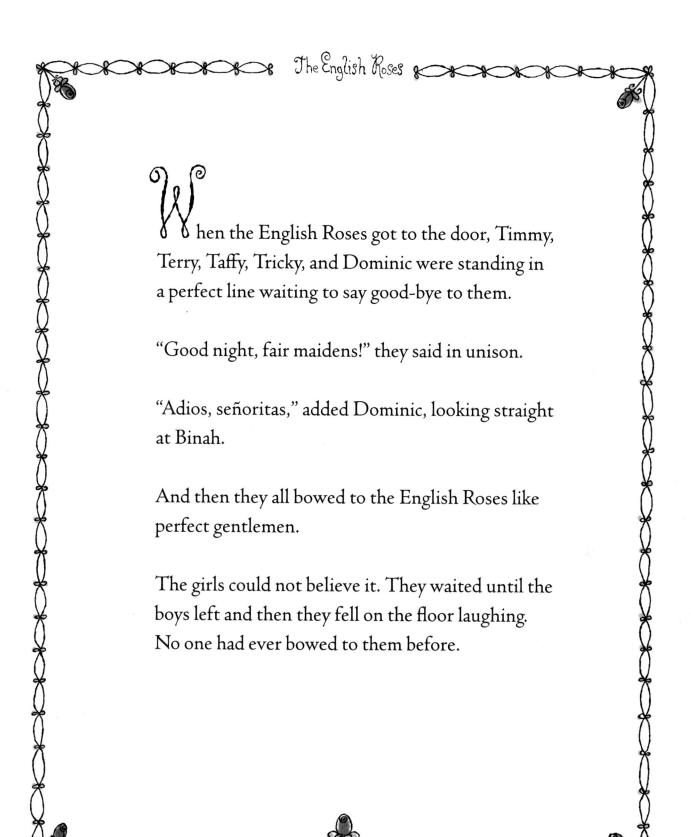

When the English Roses got to the door, Timmy,
Terry, Taffy, Tricky, and Dominic were standing in
a perfect line waiting to say good-bye to them.

"Good night, fair maidens!" they said in unison.

"Adios, señoritas," added Dominic, looking straight
at Binah.

And then they all bowed to the English Roses like
perfect gentlemen.

The girls could not believe it. They waited until the
boys left and then they fell on the floor laughing.
No one had ever bowed to them before.

The English Roses walked home together arm in arm. They apologized to Binah for being envious of her because of Dominic. They admitted that they had not been good friends to her.

Binah smiled and said, "I forgive you. We all make mistakes."

Then she poked Grace and joked, "And who knows? One day I might act like a twit and you will have to forgive me, too."

"Friends for life!" they exclaimed.

One by one they arrived at their houses.

First Charlotte,

then Amy,

then Nicole,

then Grace,

and finally, Binah.

As she walked to the door of her house, she saw her father waiting for her.

"Papa, I had such a good time tonight," she said as he gave her a big bear hug.

"That's wonderful," he said. "Tell me about it!"

"Well, first of all, Miss Fluffernutter is the coolest. Second of all, I learned how to do an Irish jig. And third of all, you can't just love your friends when they are nice to you. That's when it's easy. You have to love them when they are being complete dorks, too. Sooner or later, they'll come around."

Binah's father took her face in his hands and looked at her with so much love in his eyes. He knew her mother would be very proud of her, too. "I'd say that was quite an evening."

"Yeah, it was T.G.T.B.T.," said Binah, kissing her papa on the nose and floating up the stairs to her bedroom.

Lesson # 151 — Love your Friends

She hung up her pretty new dress
and fell fast asleep.

Produced and published by

CALLAWAY ARTS & ENTERTAINMENT

19 FULTON STREET, FIFTH FLOOR
NEW YORK, NEW YORK 10038

Nicholas Callaway, President and Publisher
Cathy Ferrara, Managing Editor and Production Director
Toshiya Masuda, Art Director · Nelson Gómez, Director of Digital Technology
Joya Rajadhyaksha, Associate Editor · Amy Cloud, Associate Editor
Ivan Wong, Jr. and José Rodríguez, Production · Krupa Jhaveri, Designer
Kathryn Bradwell, Executive Assistant to the Publisher

Special thanks to Jeffrey Fulvimari.

Distributed in the United States by Viking Children's Books.

Callaway Arts & Entertainment, its Callaway logotype, and Callaway Editions, Inc., are trademarks.

Fluffernutter is a registered trademark of Durkee-Mower, Inc. and is used by permission. All rights reserved.

ISBN 0-670-06147-6

Library of Congress Cataloging-in-Publication Data available upon request.

10 9 8 7 6 5 4 3 2 1 06 07 08 09

Printed in the United States of America

Visit Madonna at www.madonna.com   Visit Callaway at www.callaway.com

All of Madonna's proceeds from this book will be donated to Raising Malawi (www.raisingmalawi.org), an orphan-care initiative.

A NOTE ON THE TYPE:

This book is set in Mazarin, a "humanist" typeface designed by Jonathan Hoefler. Mazarin is a revival of the typeface
of Nicolas Jenson, the fifteenth-century typefounder who created one of the first roman printing types.
Copyright © 1991-2000, The Hoefler Type Foundry.

FIRST EDITION